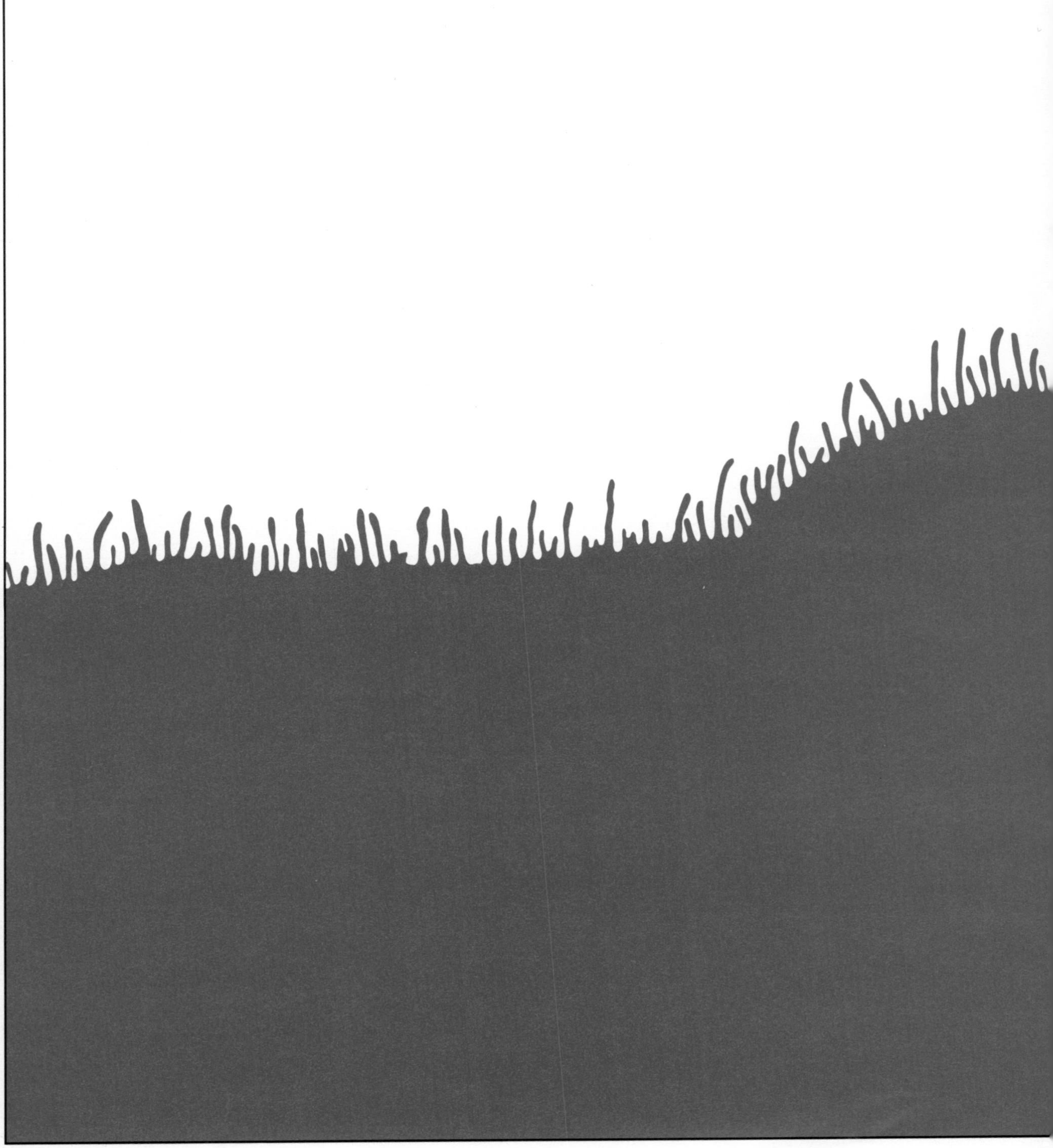

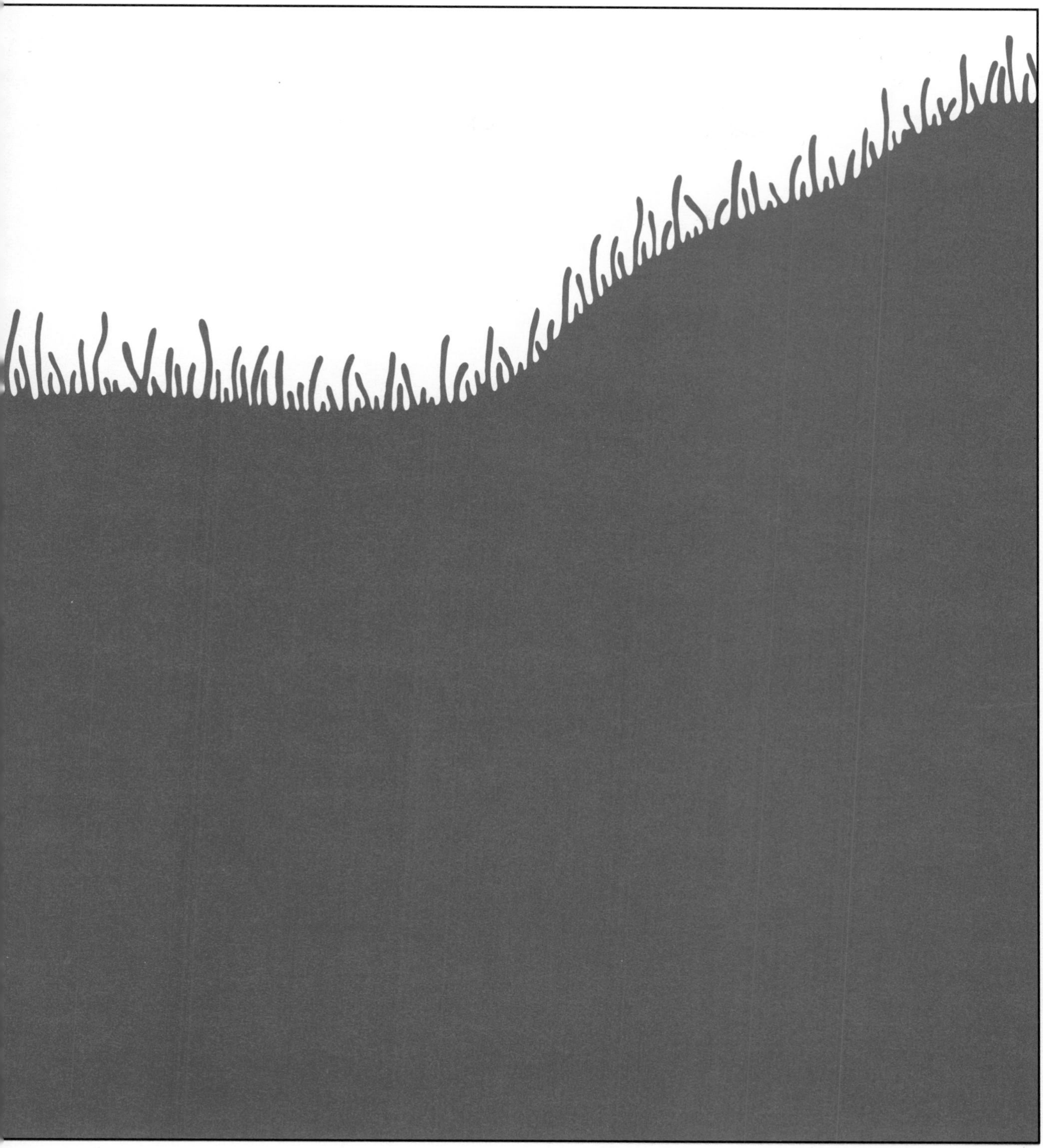

For Amy, Nina, Don, Cuddles + Teh-bear

Two Bear Cubs, by Ann Jonas. Copyright © 1982 by Ann Jonas. Reprinted by permission of Greenwillow Books, a division of William Morrow & Company, Inc.

Houghton Mifflin Edition, 1996
Copyright © 1996 by Houghton Mifflin Company. All rights reserved.

Printed in the U.S.A.

ISBN: 0-395-75354-6

23456789-B-99 98 97 96 95

Two Bear Cubs

Ann Jonas

HOUGHTON MIFFLIN COMPANY

BOSTON

ATLANTA   DALLAS   GENEVA, ILLINOIS   PALO ALTO   PRINCETON

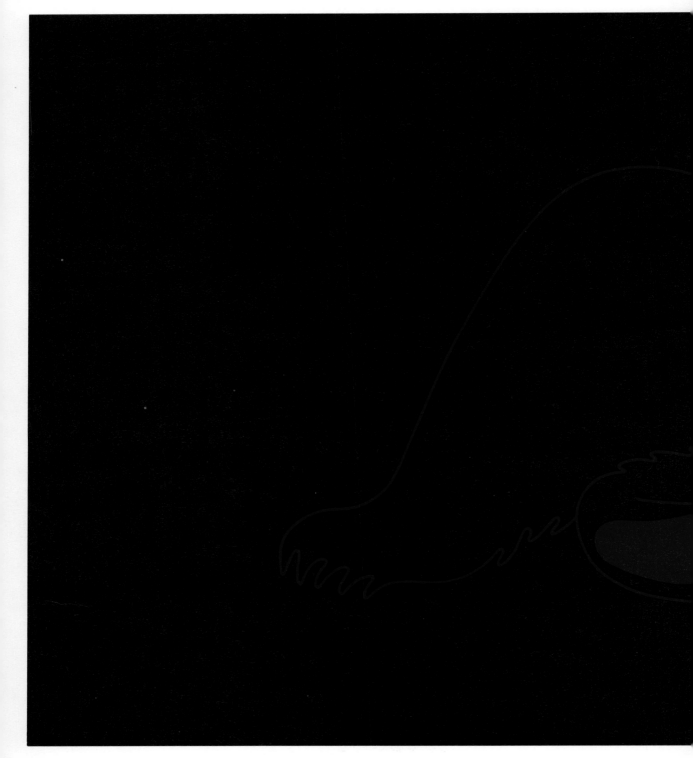

Six bright eyes look out of a dark cave.

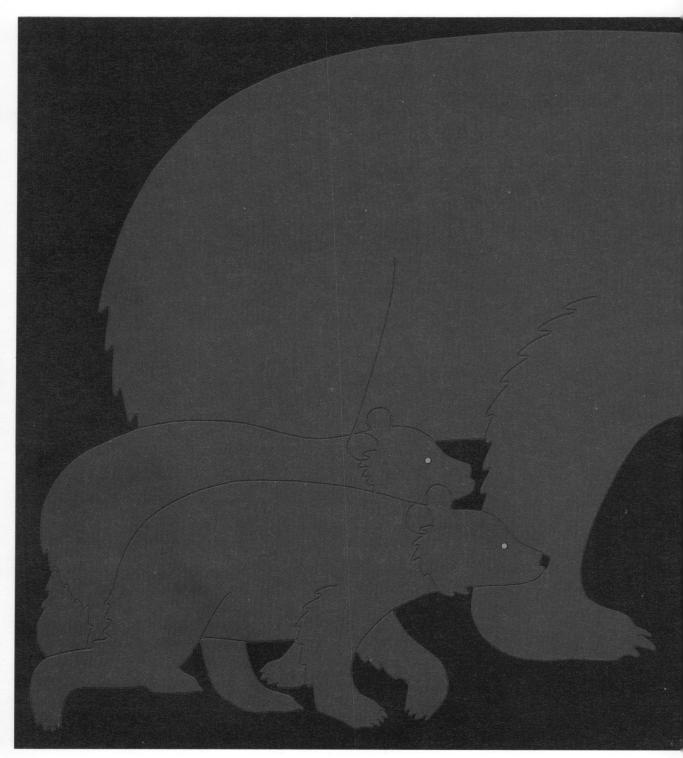

A bear and her cubs begin their day.

The mother watches while her cubs play.

**Something walks by.
It doesn't smell like a bear.**

The cubs follow it.

It follows them!

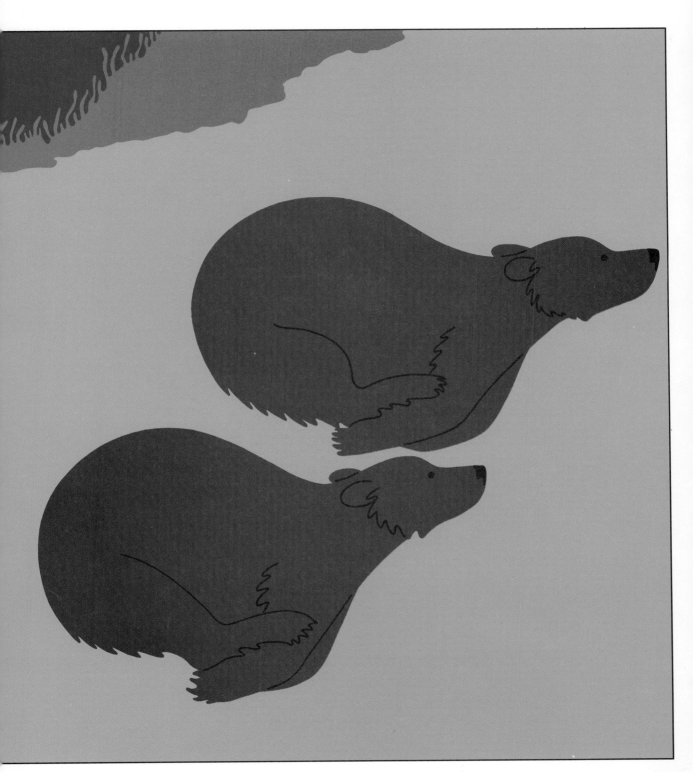

At last they outrun it.
            But where are they?

And where is their mother?

They look around.
        They sniff the ground.

No mother.

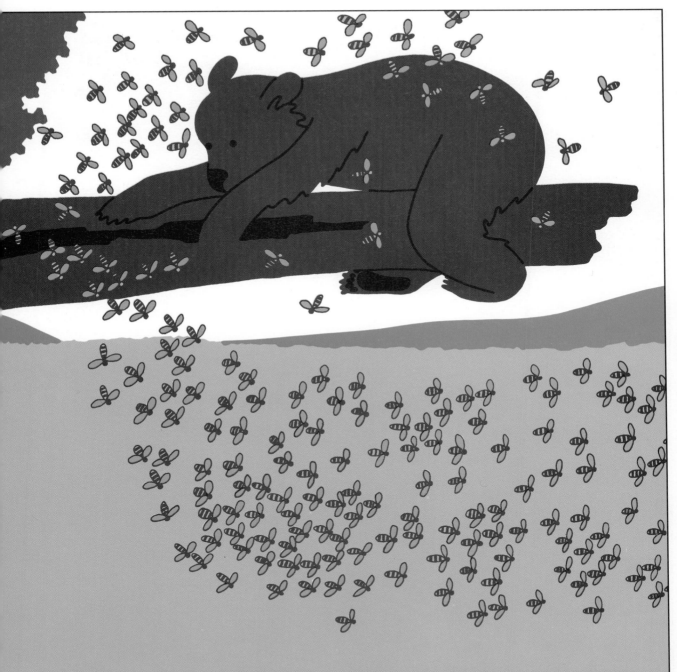

They find a honey tree all by themselves—

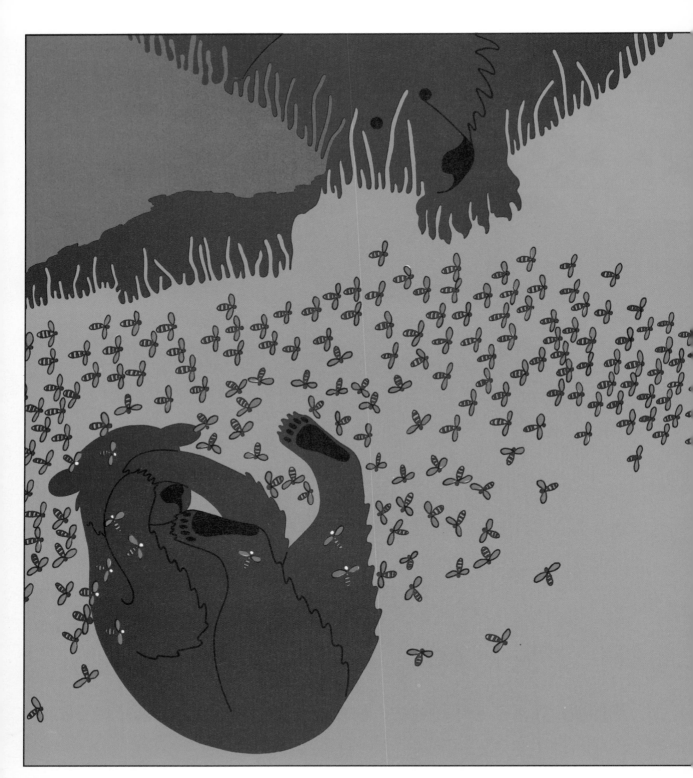

and a lot of angry bees!
Where is their mother?

They can't even catch a fish.
Where can their mother be?

There she is!

And they aren't even very far from home.

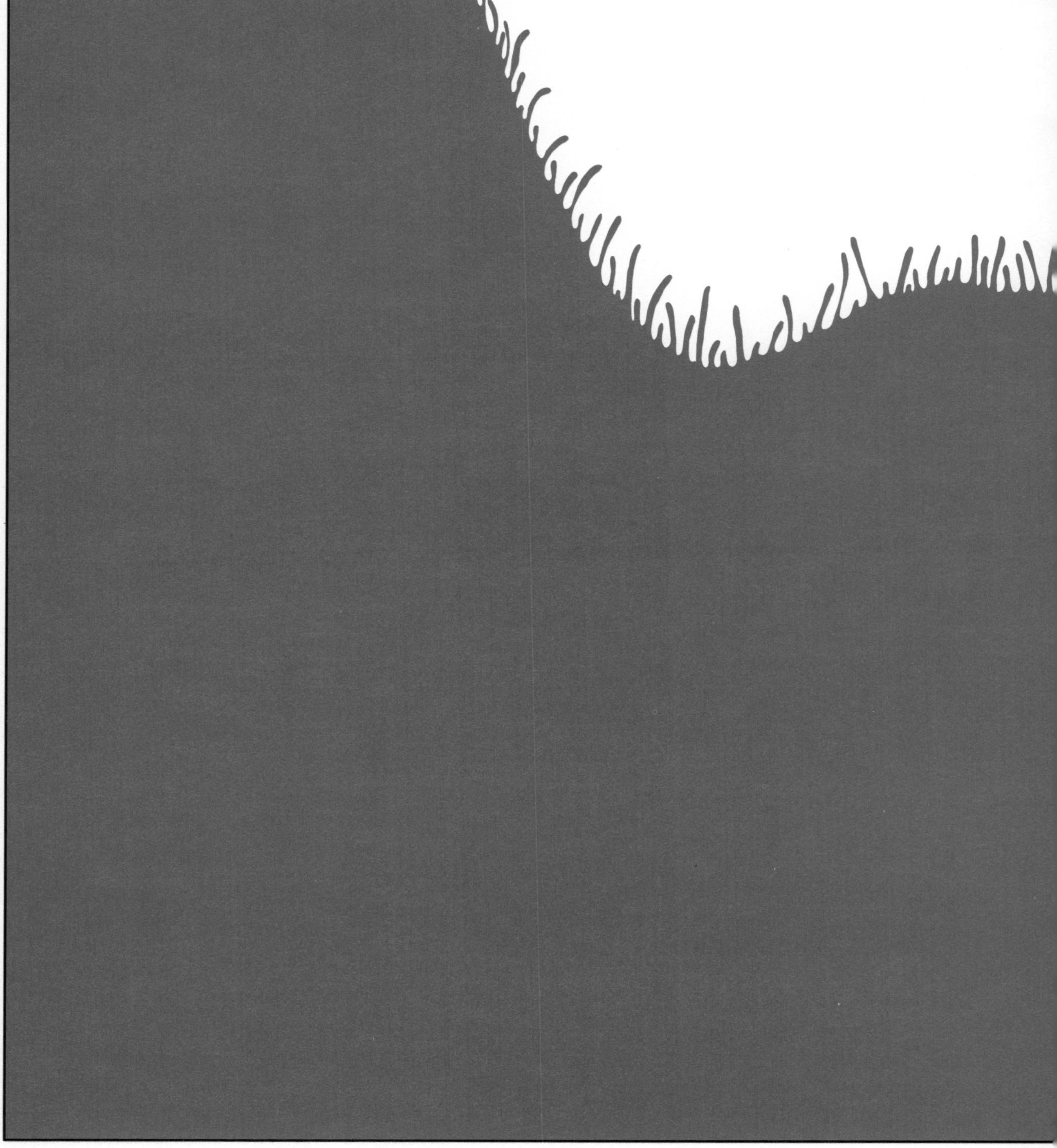

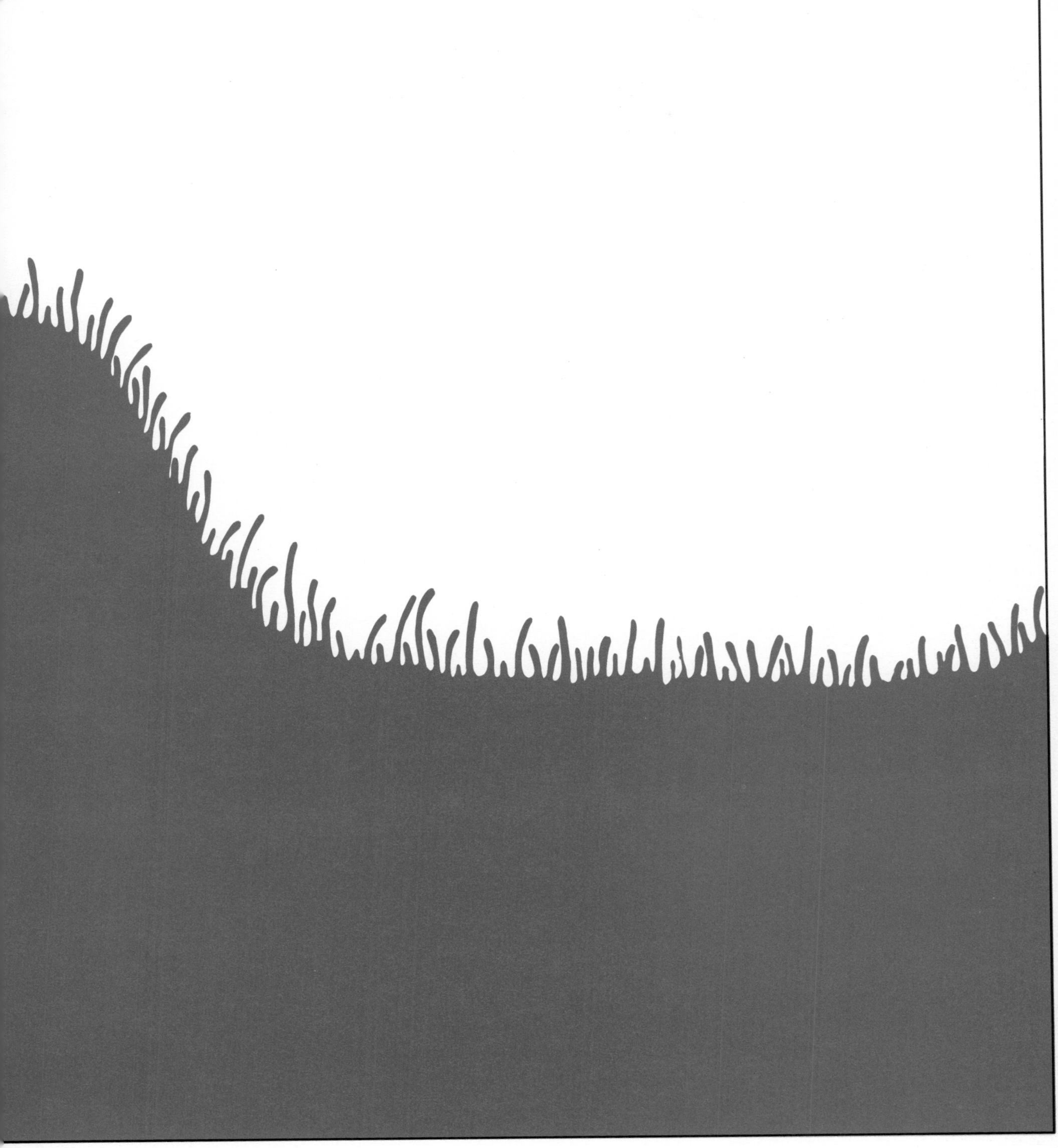